MW01136496

JAN 2019

ANIMALS OF THE RAIN FOREST

Jaguars

by Rachel Grack

BLASTOFF! READERS
2

BELLWETHER MEDIA · MINNEAPOLIS, MN

Note to Librarians, Teachers, and Parents:

Blastoff! Readers are carefully developed by literacy experts and combine standards-based content with developmentally appropriate text.

Level 1 provides the most support through repetition of high-frequency words, light text, predictable sentence patterns, and strong visual support.

Level 2 offers early readers a bit more challenge through varied simple sentences, increased text load, and less repetition of high-frequency words.

Level 3 advances early-fluent readers toward fluency through increased text and concept load, less reliance on visuals, longer sentences, and more literary language.

Level 4 builds reading stamina by providing more text per page, increased use of punctuation, greater variation in sentence patterns, and increasingly challenging vocabulary.

Level 5 encourages children to move from "learning to read" to "reading to learn" by providing even more text, varied writing styles, and less familiar topics.

Whichever book is right for your reader, Blastoff! Readers are the perfect books to build confidence and encourage a love of reading that will last a lifetime!

This edition first published in 2019 by Bellwether Media, Inc.

No part of this publication may be reproduced in whole or in part without written permission of the publisher. For information regarding permission, write to Bellwether Media, Inc., Attention: Permissions Department, 6012 Blue Circle Drive, Minnetonka, MN 55343.

Library of Congress Cataloging-in-Publication Data

Names: Koestler-Grack, Rachel A., 1973- author.
Title: Jaguars / by Rachel Grack.
Description: Minneapolis, MN : Bellwether Media, Inc., 2019. |
  Series: Blastoff! Readers. Animals of the Rain Forest | Audience: Ages 5-8. |
  Audience: K to grade 3. | Includes bibliographical references and index.
Identifiers: LCCN 2018031004 (print) | LCCN 2018037249 (ebook) |
  ISBN 9781681036748 (ebook) | ISBN 9781626179509 (hardcover : alk. paper)
Subjects: LCSH: Jaguar--Juvenile literature. | Rain forest animals--Juvenile literature.
Classification: LCC QL737.C23 (ebook) | LCC QL737.C23 K638 2019 (print) | DDC 599.75/5--dc23
LC record available at https://lccn.loc.gov/2018031004

Editor: Betsy Rathburn   Designer: Jeffrey Kollock

Printed in the United States of America, North Mankato, MN

Table of Contents

Life in the Rain Forest

Jaguars are some of the biggest wild cats in the world. They **adapted** to become top rain forest **predators**!

4

They prowl the forests of Central and South America. Long tails help them balance in tall trees.

Jaguar Range

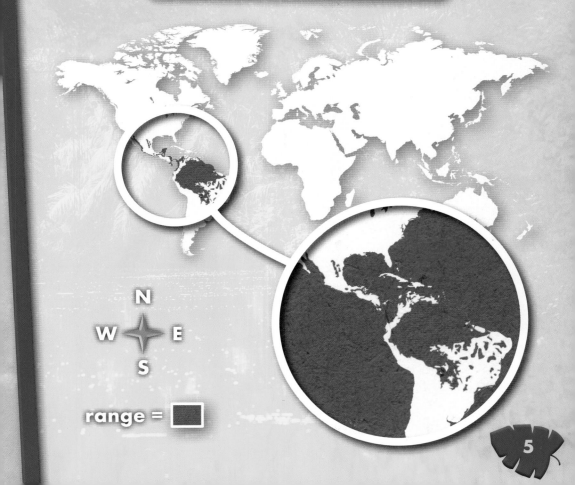

N

W E

S

range = ☐

Many plants grow in the **humid** rain forest **biome**. Jaguars hide among them.

Their orange fur is covered with black markings. Spotted coats provide **camouflage**!

Jaguars have strong legs and sharp claws. Their paws have soft pads on the bottom.

Special Adaptations

spotted fur

long tail

sharp claws

They can creep through the forest without making a sound!

Roaming Free

These big cats need
room to roam.
The rain forest
has a lot of space.

They claw trees to
mark their **territories**.
This keeps other
animals away!

Their large territories mean jaguars can live far from one another.

They have a loud roar
to **communicate** over
long distances.

Rain forests get hot!
Jaguars rest in shade
during the day.

Sometimes, they swim to cool off!

On the Hunt

These **nocturnal** hunters slowly follow **prey**. When close enough, jaguars pounce!

Deer and capybaras are favorite meals of these **carnivores**.

Jaguar Stats

| Least Concern | Near Threatened | Vulnerable | Endangered | Critically Endangered | Extinct in the Wild | Extinct |

conservation status: near threatened

life span: up 15 years

17

Jaguar jaws are two times
stronger than lion jaws.
They easily crush the skulls of prey.

Their sharp teeth can crack open turtle shells!

Jaguar Diet

marsh deer

wild pigs

capybaras

Jaguars **lure** fish by dipping their tails in water. When fish come near, big paws scoop up the meal.

The rain forest gives these big cats a big menu!

Glossary

adapted—changed over a long period of time

biome—a large area with certain plants, animals, and weather

camouflage—coloring or markings that make animals look like their surroundings

carnivores—animals that only eat meat

communicate—to share information and feelings

humid—hot and wet

lure—to draw in

nocturnal—active at night

predators—animals that hunt other animals for food

prey—animals that are hunted by other animals for food

territories—land areas where animals live

To Learn More

AT THE LIBRARY

Arnold, Quinn M. *Jaguars*. Mankato, Minn.: Creative Education, 2017.

Kenan, Tessa. *It's a Jaguar!* Minneapolis, Minn.: Lerner Publications, 2017.

Schuh, Mari. *Jaguars*. Minneapolis, Minn.: Bullfrog Books, 2015.

ON THE WEB

FACTSURFER

Factsurfer.com gives you a safe, fun way to find more information.

1. Go to www.factsurfer.com.

2. Enter "jaguars" into the search box.

3. Click the "Surf" button and select your book cover to see a list of related web sites.

Index

The images in this book are reproduced through the courtesy of: bluehand, front cover, p. 1; milosk50, pp. 4-5; Leonardo Mercon, pp. 6, 14-15; Prisma by Dukas Presseagentur GmbH/ Alamy, pp. 6-7; Kerry Manson, pp. 8-9; Kris Wiktor, pp. 9, 10-11, 20-21 (left), 22; Waitandshoot, p. 9 (inset); Mikadun, p. 10; kongsak sumano, pp. 12-13; Octavio Campos Salles/ Alamy, p. 13; Thorsten Spoerlein, p. 14; Steve Winter/ Getty Images, p. 16; nwdph, pp. 16-17; Adalbert Dragon, pp. 18-19; buteo, p. 19 (top left); kyslynskahal, p. 19 (top right); Christian Musat, p. 19 (bottom); Bill Peaslee, pp. 20-21 (right).